A NOTE TO PARENTS

When your children are ready to "step into reading," giving them the right books is as crucial as giving them the right food to eat. **Step into Reading Books** present exciting stories and information reinforced with lively, colorful illustrations that make learning to read fun, satisfying, and worthwhile. They are priced so that acquiring an entire library of them is affordable. And they are beginning readers with a difference—they're written on five levels.

Early Step into Reading Books are designed for brand-new readers, with large type and only one or two lines of very simple text per page. **Step 1 Books** feature the same easy-to-read type as the Early Step into Reading Books, but with more words per page. **Step 2 Books** are both longer and slightly more difficult, while **Step 3 Books** introduce readers to paragraphs and fully developed plot lines. **Step 4 Books** offer exciting nonfiction for the increasingly independent reader.

The grade levels assigned to the five steps—preschool through kindergarten for the Early Books, preschool through grade 1 for Step 1, grades 1 through 3 for Step 2, grades 2 through 3 for Step 3, and grades 2 through 4 for Step 4—are intended only as guides. Some children move through all five steps very rapidly; others climb the steps over a period of several years. Either way, these books will help your child "step into reading" in style!

For my daughter, Molly Rose DeVries,
with SO much love!
—D.H.

To my friend Deborah
—S.W.

Text copyright © 2000 by Deborah Hautzig. Illustrations copyright © 2000 by Sylvie Wickstrom. All rights reserved under International and Pan-American Copyright Conventions. Published in the United States by Random House, Inc., New York, and simultaneously in Canada by Random House of Canada Limited, Toronto.

www.randomhouse.com/kids

Library of Congress Cataloging-in-Publication Data
Hautzig, Deborah.
Little Witch's bad dream / by Deborah Hautzig ; illustrated by Sylvie Wickstrom.
p. cm. — (Step into reading. A step 2 book)
SUMMARY: Little Witch tries to be nice to her guest Cousin Bossy, but everything she does is wrong because witches are supposed to be bad and mean.
ISBN 0-679-87342-2 (pbk.) — ISBN 0-679-97342-7 (lib. bdg.)
[1. Witches—Fiction. 2. Behavior—Fiction. 3. Cousins—Fiction.]
I. Wickstrom, Sylvie, ill. II. Title. III. Series: Step into reading. Step 2 book. PZ7.H2888Lih
2000 [Fic]—dc21 99-20135

Printed in the United States of America July 2000 10 9 8 7 6 5 4 3 2 1

STEP INTO READING, RANDOM HOUSE, and the Random House colophon are registered trademarks and the Step into Reading colophon is a trademark of Random House, Inc.

Step into Reading®

Little Witch's Bad Dream

by Deborah Hautzig

illustrated by Sylvie Wickstrom

A Step 2 Book

Random House 🏠 New York

Little Witch was so excited!

Cousin Bossy was coming to visit.

Little Witch had made a sign.

It said: WELCOME COUSIN BOSSY!

Next, Little Witch picked flowers.

"Mother Witch won't miss them,"

she told her cat, Bow-Wow.

"She hates pretty flowers!"

Little Witch put the flowers
in a jar with water.
She took it to
Cousin Bossy's room.
"This room is a mess!"
she said to her bat, Scrubby.
"Will you help me clean it up?"

Scrubby scrubbed the walls

and ate the spiders.

Little Witch swept and dusted.

"And now for the final touch."
Little Witch took some candy from
her lunch box.
"Mother Witch gives me
SO much candy.
I never eat it all!"

Little Witch put the candy
on Cousin Bossy's pillow
with a note.
It said: SWEET DREAMS!

Mother Witch came looking

for Little Witch.

She saw the flowers,

the clean room,

the candy,

and the note.

"LITTLE WITCH!" she screeched.

"What have you DONE?"

"I'm making things nice

for Cousin Bossy,"

said Little Witch.

Mother Witch tore at her hair.

"STOP BEING SO NICE!" she wailed.

"I'll try," said Little Witch.

Little Witch sat on the porch

to wait for Cousin Bossy.

She waited,

and waited,

and waited.

"Where is she?" cried Little Witch.

"She's late," said Mother Witch.

Finally, Little Witch could not wait anymore.

She said a magic spell:

"Rushety gushety,

Lickety-split,

Get here now,

Or I'll have a fit!"

THUMP!

Cousin Bossy landed

on the porch.

"HURRAY!" shouted Little Witch.

She gave Cousin Bossy

a big hug.

"Look at the sign I made!"

"How nice!" said Cousin Bossy.

"Let me fix it."

She took Little Witch's sign
and moved it up.

"There, that looks much better."

Little Witch felt awful.

But she smiled sweetly and said,

"Yes, it does!"

Aunt Nasty and Aunt Grouchy

came to the door.

"Why are YOU here?"

grumbled Aunt Grouchy.

"I've come to visit!"

said Cousin Bossy.

"When are you leaving?"

asked Aunt Nasty.

"Tomorrow," said Cousin Bossy.

"GOOD!" screamed Aunt Nasty

and Aunt Grouchy.

Little Witch took Cousin Bossy
to her room.

Cousin Bossy took the flowers
out of the jar.

Then she put them back.

"That's better," she said.

She scrubbed the clean walls

and swept the clean floor.

"Much better!" said Cousin Bossy.

"But I already cleaned!"

Little Witch whispered sadly.

Cousin Bossy did not hear her.

Mother Witch was in the kitchen

making dinner.

"Cousin Dippy!" yelled

Mother Witch.

"Tell everyone dinner is ready!"

"Okay," said Cousin Dippy.

"YOO-HOO!" screamed Cousin Dippy.

"Breakfast time!"

Little Witch smiled.

"Cousin Dippy is all mixed up,"
Little Witch said.

"Let's eat dinner!"
She took Cousin Bossy
down to the dining room.

Everyone sat down.

"Have some cereal!"

said Cousin Dippy.

"Don't be stupid," said Aunt Nasty.

"This goop soup stinks,"

said Aunt Grouchy.

"So next time, YOU COOK!"

screamed Mother Witch.

Cousin Bossy pulled a bag

out of her pocket.

"I always bring my own food,"

she said.

"Hmmmph," growled Mother Witch.

"I left a surprise on your pillow
for dessert!" Little Witch told
Cousin Bossy.
"I don't like surprises," she said.
"You'll like this one!"
said Little Witch
with a twinkle in her eye.

After dinner,

everyone played Old Maid.

"No one goes to bed until I win!"

said Cousin Bossy.

At last, she did.

"Good night!" said Little Witch.

Everybody went upstairs.

"AAAH!" screamed Cousin Bossy.

Little Witch came running.

"This note says 'Sweet Dreams!'"

snapped Cousin Bossy.

"Don't tell me

what kind of dreams to have!

And take away this candy!"

Little Witch took the candy
and gave it to Bow-Wow.
Then she went back to bed.
"Everything I do is wrong,"
she said sadly.
It took her a long time
to fall asleep.
While she was sleeping,
Little Witch had a dream.

In the dream,

Little Witch made a sign

for Cousin Bossy.

It said: NOT WELCOME!

She put poison ivy

in Cousin Bossy's bed.

"Now if she comes, she'll itch!"

said Little Witch.

Cousin Bossy came early!

Little Witch said a spell:

"Bickery stickery,

Bossy creep,

Turn into

A garbage heap!"

POOF! Cousin Bossy

turned into a pile of

smelly garbage.

"Oh, no!" cried Little Witch.

She yelled and yelled.

Mother Witch came running.

"What's wrong?" she asked.

Little Witch sat up.

Then she began to cry.

"Something terrible happened!"
said Little Witch.

"I was MEAN! I was BAD!
I turned Cousin Bossy into
GARBAGE!"

"It was just a bad dream,"

said Mother Witch.

"So nothing bad <u>really</u> happened?"

asked Little Witch.

"NO!" yelled Mother Witch.

"A dream is not real.

I want you to be bad and mean

when you are AWAKE!"

Mother Witch hugged

Little Witch.

"Go back to sleep," she said.

"See you in the morning."

The next morning,

Little Witch ran to

Cousin Bossy's room.

"You're still here!"

cried Little Witch happily.

"Of course I am.

Where else would I be?"

said Cousin Bossy.

"BREAKFAST IS READY!"

screamed Mother Witch.

Cousin Bossy and Little Witch

ran to the table.

"Hurray! Lunch!" said Cousin Dippy.

"Oh, shut up," said Aunt Grouchy.

"I have my own food,"
said Cousin Bossy.

"You're still here?" said Aunt Nasty.

"How is your fried ear wax?"
asked Mother Witch.

"It's great!" said Little Witch.

"You're supposed to say
it's awful!"
screamed Mother Witch.

"When will you stop
being so NICE?"

41

"Maybe in my dreams,"

said Little Witch.

"When I'm awake, I'm nice.

I can't help it."

"I know," said Mother Witch sadly.

"Do you still love me?"

asked Little Witch.

"OF COURSE I DO!"

screamed Mother Witch.

"I can't help it, either."

Cousin Bossy began to clear
the table.

"HEY! We're not done yet!"
screamed Mother Witch.

"You're a pain, Cousin Bossy,"
said Aunt Grouchy.
"I know I am,"
said Cousin Bossy.
"I can't help it, either!"
All the witches laughed
and laughed.

"Maybe Little Witch can help you

get ready to leave,"

said Mother Witch.

"Sure I can! I love to help!"

said Little Witch.

POOF!

Little Witch said these magic words:

"Blickety babka,

Blackety crow,

Your suitcase is packed

And you're ready to go!"

POOF! Cousin Bossy was on

her broomstick.

She flew off into the sky.

"Come back soon!" said Little Witch.

"But not TOO soon!" screamed

Aunt Grouchy and Aunt Nasty.

Mother Witch put her arms around
Little Witch.

"I'm glad she's gone,"
said Little Witch softly.

"I'm glad you're glad,"
said Mother Witch.

They gave each other a big hug.

DATE DUE

GAYLORD			PRINTED IN U.S.A.